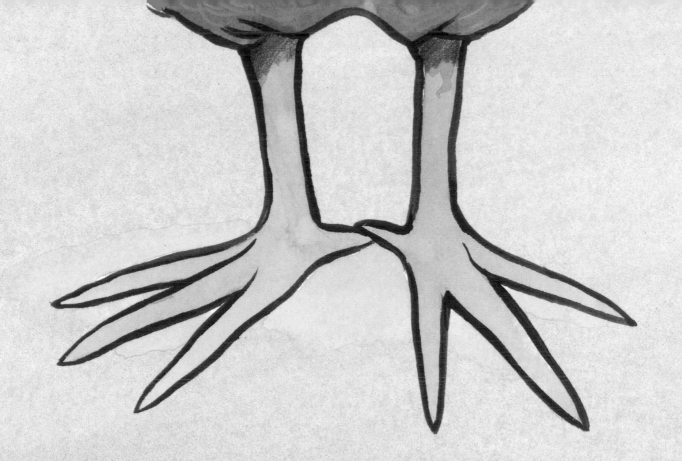

Three Hens
and a
Peacock

Dedicated to the spirit of Mr. Rogers, who always said, "I like you just the way you are."

—L. L. L.

For Winnie, with much affection

—H. C.

Published by
PEACHTREE PUBLISHERS
1700 Chattahoochee Avenue
Atlanta, Georgia 30318-2112

www.peachtree-online.com

Text © 2011 by Lester L. Laminack
Illustrations © 2011 by Henry Cole

**Illustrations created with watercolor, ink, and colored pencil on 100% rag,
archival watercolor paper.**
**Text typeset in Microsoft Corporation's Tahoma by Matthew Carter;
title typeset in Blue Vinyl Font's Meringue BV by Jess Latham.**

Printed and manufactured in May 2011 by Imago in Singapore
10 9 8 7 6 5 4 3 2

Laminack, Lester L., 1956-
** Three hens and a peacock / written by Lester L. Laminack ;
illustrated by Henry Cole.**
**   p. cm.**
** ISBN 978-1-56145-564-5 / 1-56145-564-4**
**[1. Farm life--Fiction. 2. Contentment--Fiction. 3. Peacocks--Fiction.
4. Chickens--Fiction. 5. Hounds--Fiction. 6. Dogs--Fiction.]**
I. Cole, Henry, 1955- ill. II. Title.
** PZ7.L1815Thr 2011**
** [E]--dc22**

2010031989

Three Hens and a Peacock

Written by Lester L. Laminack   Illustrated by Henry Cole

PEACHTREE
ATLANTA

Things were quiet on the Tuckers' farm.

The cows chewed their cud.

The hens clucked and pecked
and laid their eggs.

The old hound stretched out on the porch, watching and listening.

Once in a while someone would stop to buy tomatoes or corn, perhaps a quart of milk.

Nothing unusual happened there.

Until...

...that peacock showed up.

The cows and the hens and the old hound kept right on doing what they'd always done.

But that peacock had never lived on a farm. He had no idea what to do.

So he spread his fancy feathers and set to shrieking.

Eventually, the peacock wandered down to the road.

When cars whizzed by, he shook his feathers
and cried out in his loudest voice.

Of course, folks stopped for a closer look.

Day after day, more folks stopped to admire the peacock, and they all bought tomatoes and corn, eggs and milk.

Business on the Tuckers' farm was booming!

Everyone *seemed* happy to have visitors stopping by...

...but trouble was brewing in the henhouse.

The hens were squawking and clucking
and flapping their wings. "We do all the work
around here. I'd like to see that peacock lay one single egg."

"Exactly. He just struts around screaming.
I suppose *fancy feathers* are more important than *laying eggs*."

"That lazy peacock gets all the attention and we do all the work!"

The peacock had heard every word.

For days, he moped about, moaning and groaning.
"I wish I could be more useful around here."

"Humph," clucked one hen. The others ruffled their feathers.

The old hound stretched and slowly raised his head.

"Why not let the peacock
stay here to be *useful* while
you hens take the *glamorous*
job down by the road?"

The three hens began clucking to one another.

"What a wonderful plan!"

"Yes, it's a fabulous idea. Oh, ladies we simply *must* fancy up our feathers tonight. And nothing but our brightest beads, bangles, and bows."

"We'll stop traffic for sure.
Why, you girls know I can
strut with the best of them."

The peacock perked up.

"Let's do it," he declared.
"Tomorrow I'll stay here,
sit on a nest, and cluck."

"And we'll get
all gussied up,"
said the hens.
"We'll be *so*
glamorous!"

At sunrise the next morning
the hens strutted down to the road.

The peacock marched right to the henhouse and poked his head inside.

The hens flocked by the road, waiting for a car.

When they saw one approaching, they clucked and squawked and flapped their wings in a flurry of feathers. But every car whizzed right on by.

The peacock sucked in his tummy and wiggled from left to right, trying to squeeze through the tiny henhouse door.

His front half was in. His back half was out.

Down by the road, those hens
tried every chicken trick
they knew.

Still no cars stopped.

Finally, the peacock made it into the henhouse.

He held his breath and pushed with all his might, but
no matter how hard he tried he could not lay a single egg.

Not one.

The old hound stretched out
on the porch, watching and listening.

"What's that peacock doing in the
henhouse?" asked Farmer Tucker.

"Who knows," said Mrs. Tucker.
"And what are those hens doing down
by the road? Not a one of them
is up here laying eggs."

"Well, the way things are going, we aren't likely to have anyone buying eggs today," said Farmer Tucker. "We *need* that peacock down there stopping cars!"

When the peacock heard that, he smiled the
biggest smile you ever saw on a bird's beak.

I AM helping! he thought. He squirmed back and forth until he popped out of the cramped henhouse. Then he trotted off to find the hens.

The exhausted hens were all clucked out.
Every feather was out of place.

"What a day."

"We couldn't get
one car to stop."

"It's true. Why, most of them
didn't even slow down."

The peacock met the hens
as they trudged up the road.

"I can tell you I'm no good at laying eggs,"
he said. "I'm just not meant for it."

One hen nodded, "I put on my stellar strut and even *I* couldn't stop a single car," she said. "I have to hand it to you, Fancy Feathers, your job is harder than it looks."

The other hens agreed. The peacock looked relieved.

So the hens marched back to the henhouse.

The peacock strutted down to the road.

The old hound stretched out on the porch,
watching and listening.

And things were quiet again
on the Tuckers' farm.

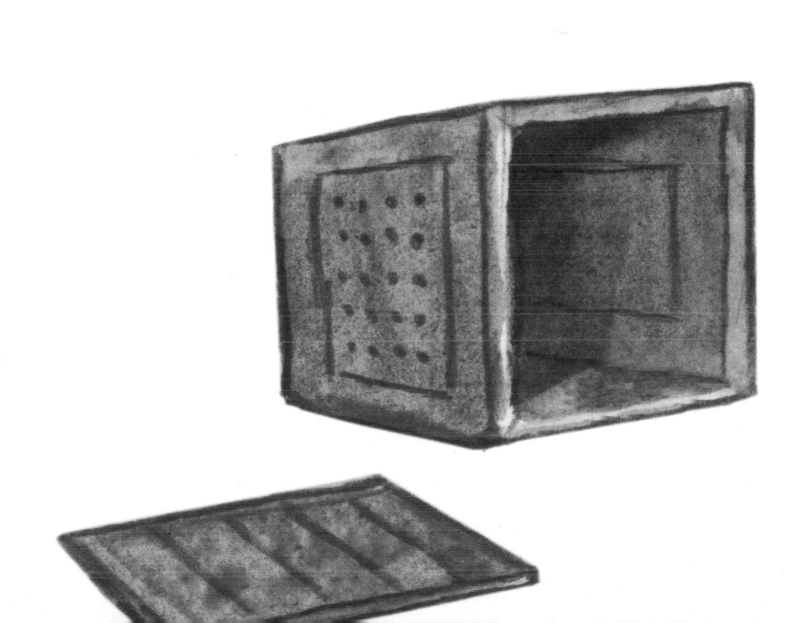

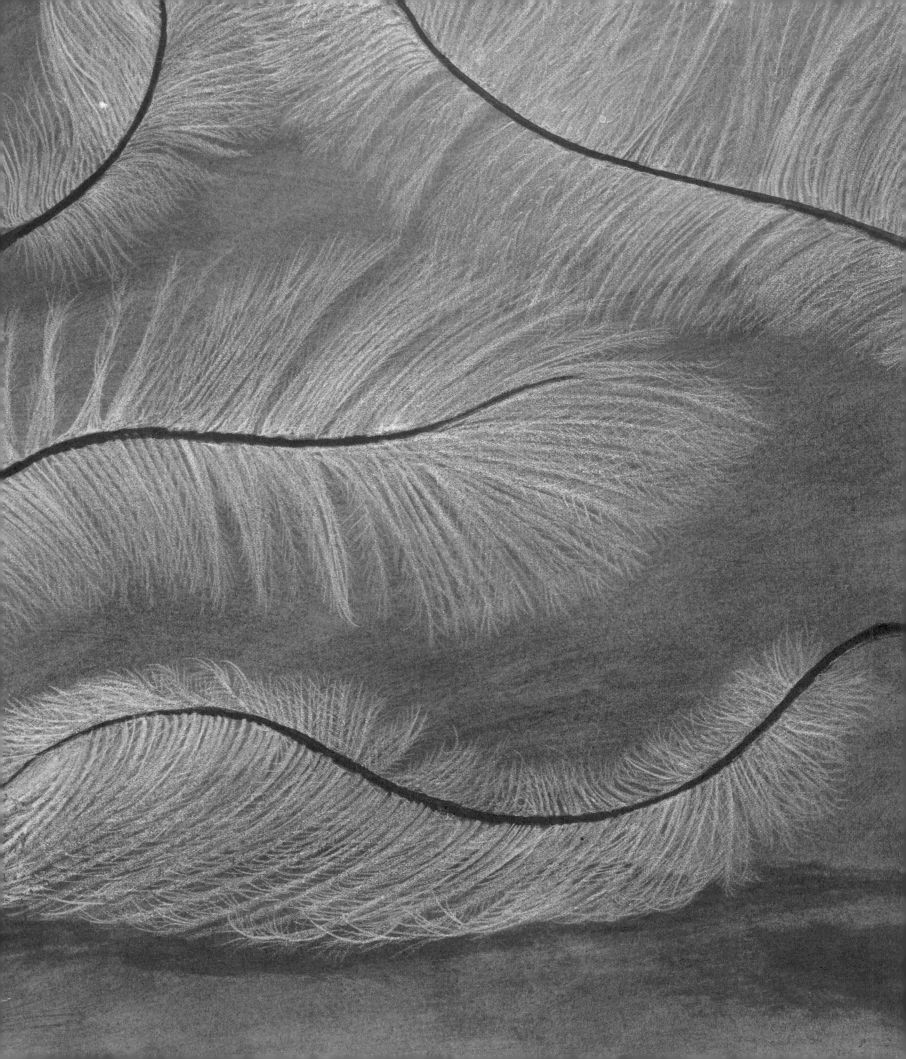